DEAN R. KOONTZ was born and raised in Pennsylvania. Even before he graduated from Shippensburg State Teacher's College, he had won an *Atlantic Monthly* fiction competition. On leaving college, he worked for a year in the Appalachian Poverty Program, continuing to write at night and during weekends, despite the tension caused by knowing that his predecessor in the job had been beaten up by the kids he was trying to help. A further eighteen months were spent teaching English in a high school near Harrisburg - and writing during the remaining hours of the week - before his wife Gerda offered to support him for five years so that he could become established as a writer. Before the five years were up, Gerda had quit her job to manage the business side of her husband's writing career. His books now sell at a rate of ten million copies a year, and are published in thirty-one languages. He has written the screenplay for the film adaptation of his novel *Midnight*, and recently wrote and was executive producer on *The Face of Fear*, a Warner Brothers-CBS Television movie. Other books by Koontz in various stages of transformation to the screen are *The Bad Place*, *Oddkins*, *Hideaway* and *Dragon Tears*. In 1976 Dean and Gerda Koontz moved to Southern California, where they still live.

THE ARTIST

Anthony Bilau

was born in Sao Paulo, Brazil, in 1962. He started work
as a professional illustrator at the age of fifteen, doing
artwork for children's books and advertising companies.
He began working the comics field in 1979. He has his
own studio and continues to work both for advertising
and publishing companies.

His favorite artists are Norman Rockwell, Bob Peak,
Neal Adams and Frank Frazetta.

THE ADAPTER

Ed Gorman

is a renowned writer of crime fiction and winner of the
Shamus Award. His novels include *The Autumn Dead*
and *The Night Remembers*. His short novel *Moon Chasers*
is being developed as a feature film. *Prisoners*, his latest
collection of stories, was called 'distinguished' by *Ellery
Queen*. About this graphic novel, Gorman writes:
'Working with Dean Koontz on *Trapped* was one of
the real high points of my career. He's the premier
storyteller of my generation.'

DEAN R. KOONTZ

TRAPPED

Illustrated by Anthony Bilau
Adapted by Ed Gorman

EclipseGraphicNovels
An Imprint of HarperCollins*Publishers*

Eclipse Graphic Novels
An Imprint of Eclipse Books and HarperCollins *Publishers*,
10 East 53rd Street
New York, N.Y. 10022   ‑

Published by Eclipse Graphic Novels 1993
First HarperPaperbacks printing: April 1993

9 8 7 6 5 4 3 2 1

Printed and bound in Hong Kong

ON THE NIGHT IT HAPPENED, A BLIZZARD SWEPT ACROSS THE ENTIRE NORTHEAST. CREATURES THAT PREFERRED TO VENTURE OUT ONLY AFTER SUNSET WERE THEREFORE DOUBLY CLOAKED BY DARKNESS AND THE STORM.

SNOW BEGAN TO FALL AT TWILIGHT, AS MEG LASSITER DROVE HOME FROM THE DOCTOR'S OFFICE WITH TOMMY. POWDERY FLAKES SIFTED OUT OF AN IRON-GRAY SKY AND AT FIRST FELL STRAIGHT DOWN THROUGH THE COLD, STILL AIR. BY THE TIME SHE COVERED EIGHT MILES, A HARD WIND SWEPT IN FROM THE SOUTHWEST.

MEG BRAKED FOR THE LAST STOPLIGHT AT THE NORTH END OF TOWN, STILL SEVEN MILES FROM THEIR FARM.

HOW OLD ARE YOU, MOM?

THIRTY-FIVE.

WOW, REALLY?

YOU MAKE IT SOUND AS IF I'M ANCIENT.

DID THEY HAVE CARS WHEN YOU WERE TEN?

HIS LAUGH WAS MUSICAL. MEG LOVED THE SOUND OF HIS LAUGHTER, PERHAPS BECAUSE SHE HAD HEARD SO LITTLE OF IT THE PAST TWO YEARS.

"COME TO THINK OF IT, HOW COULD THERE HAVE BEEN CARS WHEN YOU WERE TEN? I MEAN, GEE, THEY DIDN'T INVENT THE WHEEL TILL YOU WERE ELEVEN."

"TONIGHT FOR DINNER-- WORM CAKES AND BEETLE SOUP."

"YOU'RE THE MEANEST MOTHER IN THE WORLD."

MEG GLANCED AT TOMMY. DESPITE HIS BANTERING TONE, THE BOY WAS NOT SMILING ANY LONGER. HE WAS STARING GRIMLY AT THE TAVERN WHERE DEKE SLATER HAD BEEN DRINKING THE NIGHT HE'D KILLED JIM LASSITER. TOMMY'S FATHER.

SLIGHTLY MORE THAN TWO YEARS AGO, SLATER, DRUNK, HAD LEFT HADDENBECK'S TAVERN JUST AS NIGHT STARTED TO FALL.

AT THE SAME MO- MENT, JIM LASSITER HAD BEEN DRIVING TOWARD TOWN TO CHAIR A FUND- RAISING COMMITTEE AT ST. PAUL'S CHURCH.

TRAVELING AT A HIGH SPEED ON BLACK OAK ROAD, SLATER'S BUICK RAN HEAD-ON INTO JIM'S CAR. JIM DIED INSTANTLY, AND SLATER WAS PARALYZED FROM THE NECK DOWN, FOR LIFE.

MEG COULD NOT SEE THE BROAD MEADOWS ON EITHER SIDE, OR THE FROZEN SILVER RIBBON OF SEEGER'S CREEK OFF TO THE RIGHT, THOUGH SHE COULD MAKE OUT THE GNARLED TRUNKS AND JAGGED, WINTER-STRIPPED LIMBS OF THE LOOMING OAKS THAT FLANKED THAT PORTION OF THE COUNTRY ROAD. THE TREES WERE A LANDMARK BY WHICH SHE JUDGED THAT SHE WAS A QUARTER OF A MILE FROM THE BLIND CURVE WHERE JIM HAD DIED.

I DON'T REALLY MISS SLEDDING AND SKATING SO MUCH. IT'S JUST...I FEEL SO HELPLESS IN THIS CAST, SO...SO TRAPPED.

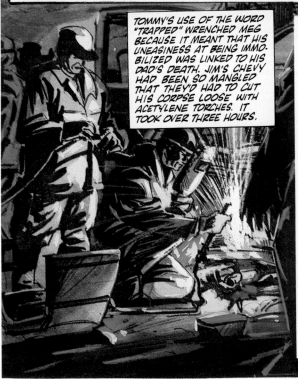

TOMMY'S USE OF THE WORD "TRAPPED" WRENCHED MEG BECAUSE IT MEANT THAT HIS UNEASINESS AT BEING IMMO-BILIZED WAS LINKED TO HIS DAD'S DEATH. JIM'S CHEVY HAD BEEN SO MANGLED THAT THEY'D HAD TO CUT HIS CORPSE LOOSE WITH ACETYLENE TORCHES. IT TOOK OVER THREE HOURS.

AT THE TIME, SHE HAD TRIED TO PROTECT TOMMY FROM THE WORST DETAILS OF THE ACCIDENT, BUT WHEN EVENTUALLY HE RETURNED TO HIS THIRD-GRADE CLASS, HIS SCHOOLMATES HAD INSISTED ON SHARING THE GRISLY FACTS WITH HIM, MO-TIVATED BY A MORBID CURIOSITY ABOUT DEATH AND BY AN INNOCENT CRUELTY PECULIAR TO SOME CHILDREN.

MEG PULLED THE STEERING WHEEL TO THE RIGHT, SWINGING ONTO HARD SHOULDER, PUMPING THE BRAKES, AFRAID OF PUTTING TWO WHEELS IN A DITCH AND ROLLING THE WAGON.

SHE HELD IT ALL THE WAY AROUND THE CURVE, HOWEVER, AS THE TIRES CHURNED UP CHUNKS OF GRAVEL THAT RATTLED AGAINST THE UNDERCARRIAGE.

IDIOT!

YOU OKAY?

Y-YEAH. OKAY.

I'D LIKE TO GET MY HANDS ON THAT IRRESPONSIBLE JERK.

IT WAS A BIOLOMECH CAR. I SAW THE NAME ON THE SIDE.

YOU SURE YOU'RE OKAY?

I JUST... WANT TO GET HOME.

BACK ON BLACK OAK ROAD, THEY CRAWLED ALONG AT TWENTY-FIVE MILES AN HOUR. WEATHER CONDITIONS WOULDN'T PERMIT GREATER SPEED.

TWO MILES FARTHER, AT BIOLOMECH, STRANGE LIGHTS FILLED THE NIGHT. BEYOND THE NINE-FOOT-HIGH, CHAIN-LINK FENCE THAT RINGED THE PLACE, SODIUM VAPOR SECURITY LAMPS GLOWED EERILY ATOP TWENTY-FOOT POLES. MEG HAD SEEN THEM BURNING ON ONLY ONE OTHER NIGHT IN FOUR YEARS.

PAIRS OF MEN IN HEAVY COATS MOVED ALONG THE PERIMETER OF THE PROPERTY, SWEEPING FLASHLIGHTS AND THE INTENSE BEAMS OF HAND-HELD SPOTLIGHTS OVER THE FENCE, AS IF LOOKING FOR A BREACH, FOCUSING ESPECIALLY ON THE SNOW-MANTLED GROUND ALONG THE CHAIN LINK.

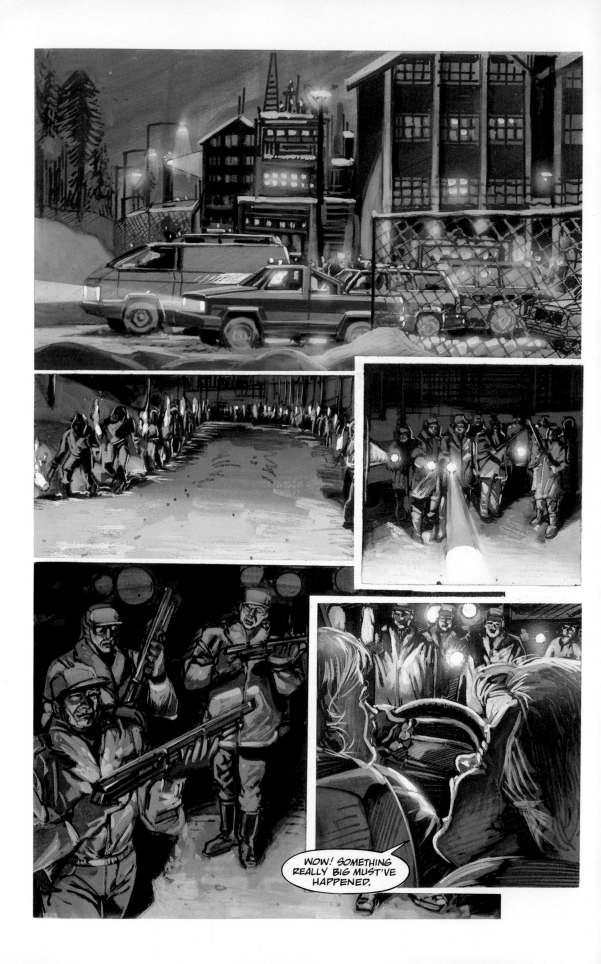

MEG ROLLED DOWN HER WINDOW. SHE EXPECTED ONE OF THE MEN TO APPROACH HER.

THEY'RE LOOKING FOR BOMBS!

BOMBS? HARDLY.

BIOLOMECH WAS INVOLVED IN RECOMBINANT-DNA RESEARCH AND THE APPLICATION OF THEIR DISCOVERIES TO COMMERCIAL ENTERPRISE.

MEG KNEW THAT IN RECENT YEARS GENETIC ENGINEERING HAD PRODUCED A MANMADE VIRUS THAT THREW OFF PURE INSULIN AS A WASTE PRODUCT, A MULTITUDE OF WONDER DRUGS, AND OTHER BLESSINGS.

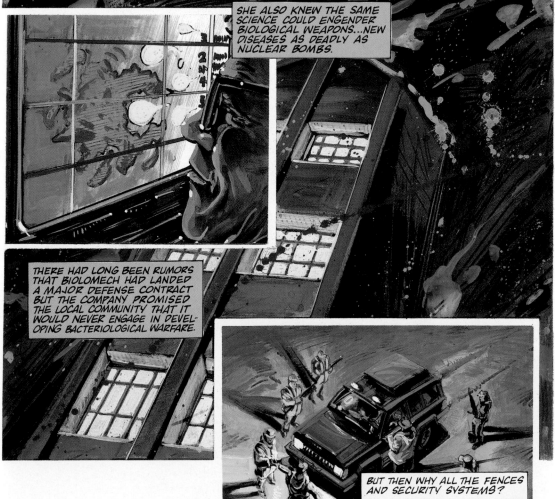

SHE ALSO KNEW THE SAME SCIENCE COULD ENGENDER BIOLOGICAL WEAPONS...NEW DISEASES AS DEADLY AS NUCLEAR BOMBS.

THERE HAD LONG BEEN RUMORS THAT BIOLOMECH HAD LANDED A MAJOR DEFENSE CONTRACT BUT THE COMPANY PROMISED THE LOCAL COMMUNITY THAT IT WOULD NEVER ENGAGE IN DEVELOPING BACTERIOLOGICAL WARFARE.

BUT THEN WHY ALL THE FENCES AND SECURITY SYSTEMS?

YOU LIVE NEAR HERE, MRS. LASSITER?

CASCADE FARM. ABOUT A MILE DOWN THE ROAD.

YOU THINK TERRORISTS WITH BOMBS ARE GONNA DRIVE IN THERE AND BLOW THE PLACE UP OR SOMETHING?

BOMBS? WHATEVER GAVE YOU THAT IDEA, SON?

THE MIRRORS ON THE POLE.

WELL, THAT'S JUST PART OF OUR STANDARD PROCEDURE IN A SECURITY ALERT. LIKE I SAID, IT'S PROBABLY A FALSE ALARM. SHORT CIRCUIT, SOMETHING LIKE THAT.

SORRY FOR THE TROUBLE, MRS. LASSITER.

AS THE MAN STEPPED BACK FROM THE STATION WAGON, MEG GLANCED PAST HIM AT THE GUARDS WITH SHOTGUNS AND AT MORE DISTANT FIGURES COMBING THE EERILY LIGHTED GROUNDS.

THESE MEN DID NOT BELIEVE THEY WERE INVESTIGATING A FALSE ALARM. THEIR ANXIETY AND TENSION WERE VISIBLE NOT ONLY IN THE FACES OF THOSE NEARBY BUT IN THE WAY ALL OF THEM STOOD AND MOVED IN THE BLIZZARD-SHOT NIGHT.

YOU THINK HE WAS LYING?

IT'S NONE OF OUR BUSINESS, HONEY.

TERRORISTS OR RUSSIANS.

CASCADE FARM WAS A TEN-ACRE SPREAD IN SEMI-RURAL CONNECTICUT. IT WAS NOT A WORKING FARM ANY MORE. MEG AND JIM HAD BOUGHT THE PLACE FOUR YEARS AGO, AFTER HE SOLD HIS SHARE IN THE NEW YORK AD AGENCY THAT HE'D FOUNDED WITH TWO PARTNERS.

THE FARM WAS TO HAVE BEEN THE START OF A NEW LIFE, WHERE HE COULD PURSUE HIS DREAM OF BEING A WRITER OF MORE THAN JUST AD COPY, AND MEG COULD ENJOY AN ART STUDIO MORE SPACIOUS AND IN A MORE SERENE ENVIRONMENT THAN ANYTHING SHE COULD HAVE HAD IN THE CITY.

BEN PARNELL PULLED UP TO LAB 3, THE BUILDING DEEPEST IN THE BIOLOMECH COMPLEX.

IN A STRANGE WAY, HE WAS GLAD THAT THE CRISIS HAD ARISEN.

IF HE HAD NOT BEEN THERE, HE WOULD HAVE BEEN AT HOME, ALONE, PRETENDING TO READ, PRETENDING TO WATCH TV, BUT BROODING ABOUT MELISSA, HIS MUCH-LOVED DAUGHTER, WHO WAS GONE, LOST TO CANCER. OR BROODING INSTEAD ABOUT LEAH, HIS WIFE, WHO HAD ALSO BEEN LOST TO...WHAT?

HE STILL DID NOT FULLY UNDERSTAND WHY THEIR MARRIAGE HAD ENDED AFTER THE ORDEAL WITH MELISSA WAS OVER.

AS FAR AS BEN COULD SEE, THE ONLY THING THAT HAD COME BETWEEN HIM AND LEAH HAD BEEN HER GRIEF, WHICH HAD BEEN SO GREAT AND DARK AND HEAVY THAT SHE NO LONGER HAD BEEN CAPABLE OF ANY OTHER EMOTION, NOT EVEN LOVE FOR HIM.

HE STILL LOVED HER. NOT PASSIONATELY BUT IN A MELANCHOLY WAY. BUT SHE WAS NOW A DREAM, A DREAM OF WHAT COULD NEVER BE.

YES, I JUST GOT IN. GET ME ALL CRISIS REPORTS ON PROJECT BLACKBERRY IMMEDIATELY. I WANT TO KNOW STATUS... THIS IS VERY BAD.

BEN! HAVE YOU FOUND OUR RATS?

NOT A TRACE, DR. ACUFF. I WANT TO TALK TO YOU, GET SOME IDEA OF WHERE THEY WOULD GO.

"WE'VE GOT TO GET OUR HANDS ON THEM, BEN. IF WE DON'T RECOVER THEM...THE POSSIBLE CONSEQUENCES ARE TERRIFYING."

GRRR

GRRR

DOOFUS GROWLED AT WHOMEVER WAS IN THE DARKNESS BEYOND THE ARCHWAY. HE WAS NOT AN EASILY FRIGHTENED DOG.

STAY THERE.

MOM?

WHAT'S WRONG?

WHINE

SINCE JIM'S DEATH, MEG HAD BEEN PARANOID ABOUT TOMMY'S HEALTH AND SAFETY. IF SHE LOST TOMMY, SHE WOULD NOT ONLY BE LOSING HER SON BUT THE LAST LIVING PART OF JIM, AS WELL.

SHE HAD BEEN AFRAID THAT TOMMY WOULD SUCCUMB TO DISEASE OR ACCIDENT--THE BROKEN LEG HAD SCARED HER--BUT ALTHOUGH SHE HAD BOUGHT A GUN FOR PROTECTION, SHE HAD NOT GIVEN MUCH THOUGHT TO FOUL PLAY.

FOUL PLAY: THAT SOUNDED MELODRAMATIC, RIDICULOUS. YET SOMETHING HAD SHAKEN THE LABRADOR, A BREED PRIZED FOR COURAGE. IF NOT AN INTRUDER, WHAT?

DON'T BE SUCH A WIMP.

HER OWN COURAGE WAS DRAINING AWAY. SHE HAD BRAVELY GONE THROUGH THE FIRST FLOOR ROOMS, DRIVEN BY FEAR FOR TOMMY'S SAFETY. NOW SHE WONDERED WHAT SHE WOULD DO IF SHE ACTUALLY ENCOUNTERED AN INTRUDER.

THOUGH SHE HATED GUNS, HER FEAR FOR TOMMY'S SAFETY HAD LED HER TO BUY A 12-GUAGE, PISTOL-GRIP, SHORT-BARRELED MOSSBERG SHOTGUN.

BY USING LIGHTLY LOADED SHELLS, SHE COULD DETER AN AGGRESSOR WITHOUT HAVING TO DESTROY HIM. SHE DIDN'T WANT TO KILL ANYONE. SHE HATED GUNS.

SHE CHECKED OUT THE REST OF THE HOUSE-- THE GUEST ROOM, HER ART STUDIO, A SPARE WALK-IN CLOSET, TOMMY'S ROOM. NOTHING.

JIM'S OFFICE WAS THE LAST PLACE SHE CHECKED. SHE LOWERED THE SHOTGUN, COMPOSING HERSELF. AFTER JIM'S DEATH, MEG HAD LEFT HIS OFFICE UNTOUCHED. THE ROOM HELPED HER TO RECALL HOW HAPPY JIM HAD BEEN WITH A NOVEL UNDER WAY.

SINCE HIS FUNERAL SHE SOMETIMES CAME TO THIS ROOM TO SIT AND REMEMBER HIM.

OFTEN SHE FELT TRAPPED BY JIM'S DEATH, AS IF A DOOR HAD SLAMMED SHUT AND LOCKED AFTER HIM WHEN HE HAD STEPPED OUT OF HER LIFE, AS IF SHE WERE NOW IN A TINY ROOM BEHIND THAT DOOR, WITH NO KEY TO FREE HERSELF, WITH NO WINDOW BY WHICH SHE COULD ESCAPE.

HOW COULD SHE BUILD A NEW LIFE, FIND HAPPINESS AFTER LOSING A MAN SHE HAD LOVED SO DEEPLY? WHAT SHE'D HAD WITH JIM WAS PERFECTION. COULD ANY FUTURE RELATIONSHIP EQUAL IT?

A SUDDEN AND UNCANNY AWARENESS OF BEING UNDER OBSERVATION WAS SO POWERFUL THAT SHE TURNED TO LOOK BACK DOWN THE HALL. EMPTY. BESIDES, SHE HAD SEARCHED EVERYWHERE. SHE WAS CERTAIN SHE AND TOMMY WERE ALONE.

WHAT'S WRONG?

NOTHING, HONEY. THE WAY DOOFUS WAS ACTING, I THOUGHT WE HAD A BURGLAR, BUT NO ONE'S BEEN HERE.

DOOFUS WAS NO LONGER SLINKING ABOUT WITH HIS HEAD HELD LOW. HE WAS HIS OLD SELF AGAIN.

TAKE OFF YOUR COAT AND GLOVES, BUT DON'T YOU GET OUT OF THAT CHAIR UNTIL I COME BACK WITH YOUR CRUTCHES.

OKAY, PAL?

COME ON, BOY, YOU GOING TO LEAVE US IN HERE UNPROTECTED?

AS IF HE UNDERSTOOD THAT HIS REPUTATION WAS AT STAKE, DOOFUS RELUCTANTLY SLUNK ACROSS THE THRESHOLD.

HEY!

DON'T YOU DARE SHAKE YOUR COAT UNTIL I'VE DRIED YOU, POOCH.

HAHAHAHAHA

AFTER FILLING TWO DISHES WITH POISONED PELLETS, SHE PUT ONE IN THE CUPBOARD UNDER THE SINK, THE OTHER IN THE CABINET WITH THE SALTINES. SHE BAITED FOUR TRAPS WITH BEEF, PUTTING ONE IN THE CABINET UNDER THE SINK, ANOTHER IN THE CABINET WITH THE SALTINES, BUT ON A DIFFERENT SHELF. SHE PLACED THE THIRD TRAP IN THE WALK-IN PANTRY AND THE FOURTH IN THE BASEMENT.

AS SOON AS I'M DONE HERE, LET'S GO INTO THE LIVING ROOM. WE MIGHT NAIL IT TONIGHT, BUT CERTAINLY BY TOMORROW MORNING.

MEG HOPED THE DARKNESS WOULD LURE THE RAT OUT OF HIDING AND INTO A TRAP BEFORE SHE RETIRED FOR THE NIGHT. SHE WOULD SLEEP BETTER KNOWING THE THING WAS DEAD.

HALF AN HOUR LATER...

SNAP
SNAP

TWO!
WE CAUGHT
TWO AT
THE SAME
TIME!

MEG ARMED HERSELF WITH
A FIREPLACE POKER IN CASE
THE PREY NEEDED TO BE
STRUCK TO FINISH THEM
OFF. SHE **HATED** THIS PART
OF RAT CATCHING.

SHE WENT TO THE KITCHEN, SWITCHED ON THE LIGHTS, AND LOOKED FIRST IN THE CABINET BENEATH THE SINK.

IN THE DISH, THE POISONED FOOD WAS ALMOST GONE. THE BEEF WAS GONE FROM THE BIG TRAP TOO; THE STEEL BAR HAD BEEN SPRUNG, BUT NO RAT HAD BEEN CAUGHT.

HOWEVER, THE TRAP WAS NOT EMPTY. CAUGHT UNDER THE BAR WAS A SIX-INCH-LONG STICK OF WOOD, AS IF IT HAD BEEN USED TO SPRING THE TRAP SO THE BAIT COULD BE SAFELY TAKEN.

A SHIVER SHOOK HER, BUT SHE WAS RELUCTANT TO CONSIDER THE FRIGHTENING THOUGHT THAT HAD GIVEN RISE TO HER TREMORS.

THEN SHE NOTICED THE DARKISH BROWN, PEA-SIZED PELLET ON THE SHELF IN FRONT OF AN OPEN BOX OF ALL-BRAN: A PIECE OF WARFARIN BAIT. BUT SHE HAD NOT PUT ANY BAIT ON THE SHELF WITH THE CEREAL; ALL OF IT HAD BEEN IN THE DISH BELOW, OR UNDER THE KITCHEN SINK. SO A RAT HAD CARRIED A PIECE OF IT ONTO THE HIGHER SHELF.

IF SHE HADN'T BEEN ALERTED BY THE PELLET, SHE MIGHT NOT HAVE NOTICED THE SCRATCH MARKS AND SMALL PUNCTURES ON THE PACKAGE OF ALL-BRAN. HEART HAMMERING, SHE STARED AT THE BOX FOR A LONG TIME BEFORE SHE TOOK IT OFF THE SHELF AND CARRIED IT TO THE SINK.

IN THE CUPBOARD BY THE REFRIGERATOR, THE POISONED BAIT HAD BEEN TAKEN FROM THE OTHER DISH. THE SECOND TRAP HAD BEEN SPRUNG, TOO. WITH ANOTHER STICK OF PLYWOOD. THE BAIT HAD BEEN STOLEN.

WHAT KIND OF RAT WAS SMART ENOUGH...?

SHE ROSE FROM HER KNEES AND OPENED THE MIDDLE DOORS OF THAT CABINET. THE CANNED GOODS, PACKAGES OF JELL-O, BOXES OF RAISINS, AND BOXES OF CEREAL LOOKED UNDISTURBED AT FIRST.

SCREECH!

IT WAS ON THE SHELF WHERE THE ALL-BRAN HAD BEEN, STANDING ON ITS HIND QUARTERS. THE SHELF WAS FIFTEEN INCHES HIGH, AND THE RAT WAS NOT ENTIRELY ERECT BECAUSE IT WAS ABOUT EIGHTEEN INCHES LONG, SIX INCHES LONGER THAN AN AVERAGE RAT, EXCLUSIVE OF ITS TAIL.

BUT ITS SIZE WASN'T WHAT ICED HER BLOOD. THE SCARY THING WAS ITS HEAD: TWICE THE SIZE OF A RAT'S HEAD, BIG AS A BASEBALL, OUT OF PROPORTION TO ITS BODY--AND ODDLY SHAPED, BULGING TOWARD THE TOP OF THE SKULL, EYES AND NOSE AND MOUTH SQUEEZED IN THE LOWER HALF.

IT STARED AT HER AND MADE CLAWING MOTIONS WITH ITS UPRAISED FOREPAWS. IT BARED ITS TEETH AND HISSED--ACTUALLY HISSED LIKE A CAT--THEN SHRIEKED AGAIN, AND THERE WAS SUCH HOSTILITY IN ITS SHRILL CRY AND IN ITS DEMEANOR THAT SHE SNATCHED UP THE FIREPLACE POKER THAT MOMENTS AGO SHE HAD PUT DOWN ON THE KITCHEN COUNTER.

THOUGH ITS EYES WERE BEADY AND RED LIKE ANY RATS, THERE WAS A DIFFERENCE ABOUT THEM THAT SHE COULD NOT IMMEDIATELY IDENTIFY. THE WAY IT STARED AT HER SO BOLDLY WAS TERRIFYING. SHE LOOKED AT IT'S ENLARGED SKULL--THE BIGGER THE SKULL, THE BIGGER THE BRAIN--AND SUDDENLY REALIZED THAT WHAT SHE SAW IN THE SCARLET EYES WAS AN UNTHINKABLY HIGH, UNRATLIKE DEGREE OF INTELLIGENCE.

WILD RATS WEREN'T WHITE.
LAB RATS WERE WHITE.

SHE KNEW NOW WHAT THEY HAD BEEN SEARCHING FOR AT THE ROADBLOCK AT BIOLOMECH. SHE DIDN'T KNOW WHY THEIR RESEARCHERS WOULD HAVE WANTED TO CREATE SUCH A BEAST AS THIS, AND THOUGH SHE WAS A WELL-EDUCATED WOMAN AND HAD A LAYMAN'S KNOWLEDGE OF GENETIC ENGINEERING, SHE DIDN'T KNOW HOW THEY HAD CREATED IT, BUT SHE KNEW BEYOND A DOUBT THAT THEY HAD CREATED IT, FOR THERE WAS NO PLACE ELSE ON EARTH FROM WHICH IT COULD HAVE COME.

"WE DIDN'T THINK THEY'D BE SMART ENOUGH TO PICK A LOCK!"

HERE, SEE? IT LOCKS AUTOMATICALLY EVERY TIME THE DOOR IS SHUT, SO IT CAN'T BE LEFT UNLOCKED BY MISTAKE. IT CAN ONLY BE OPENED WITH A KEY.

BUT SURELY... HOW COULD THEY-- WITHOUT HANDS?

YOU EVER SEE THEIR FEET? A RAT'S FEET AREN'T LIKE HANDS, BUT THEY'RE MORE THAN JUST PAWS. THEY CAN GRASP THINGS. IT'S TRUE OF MOST RODENTS.

YES, BUT WITHOUT OPPOSABLE THUMBS...

OF COURSE, THEY DON'T HAVE GREAT DEXTERITY. BUT THESE AREN'T ORDINARY RATS. THESE CREATURES HAVE BEEN GENETICALLY ALTERED. EXCEPT FOR THEIR CRANIUMS, THEY AREN'T PHYSICALLY DIF-FERENT, BUT THEY'RE A LOT SMARTER.

ANYWAY, THERE'S THIS TO CONSIDER. THEY CHEWED UP FOOD PELLETS, THEN FILLED THE SLOT WITH PASTE, SO THE BOLT COULDN'T AUTOMAT-ICALLY ENGAGE.

WE WERE MORE INTERESTED IN WHAT THEY DID AFTER THEY ENTERED THE MAZE.

I'VE ALREADY SEEN HOW THEY GOT OUT OF THE ROOM ITSELF. WE'VE CHECKED THE EXCHANGE CHAMBER, TOO.

THE DOOR HAD TO BE OPEN...

WHEN WE ATTACH THE MAZE, THE DOOR IS LEFT OPEN. IF SOME OF THEM PAUSED AT THE DOOR BEFORE ENTERING THE MAZE, WE MIGHT NOT HAVE NOTICED.

BECAUSE OF THE NATURE OF THE WORK DONE IN LAB 3, ALL AIR PASSED THROUGH A FIVE-TIERED CHAMBER OF MULTIPLE CHEMICAL BATHS BEFORE EXITING THE BUILDING.

WE FOUND NO BODIES IN THE BATHS, AND NO OTHER DISTURBED GRILLS. WE'VE FOUND GNAWED AREAS OF SUBROOF AND SHINGLES.

ONCE ON THE ROOF, THEY COULD GET OFF THE BUILDING EASILY.

WE'VE GOT TO GET THEM BACK, BEN, NO MATTER WHAT. IF THEY BREED IN THE WILD...

RATS ALREADY TAKE A LARGE PORTION OF THE WORLD'S FOOD SUPPLY... MAYBE 10 TO 15 PERCENT IN THE DEVELOPED COUNTRIES. BEN, WE LOSE THAT MUCH TO DUMB RATS. WHAT'LL WE LOSE TO THESE? WE MIGHT EVENTUALLY SEE FAMINE, EVEN HERE IN THE STATES.

YOU'RE OVERSTATING THE DANGER.

ABSOLUTELY NOT! RATS ARE PARASITICAL. THEY'RE COMPETITORS, AND THESE ARE SCORES OF TIMES SMARTER AND MORE AGGRESSIVE. COMBINE THAT LEVEL OF INTELLECT WITH THEIR SIZE ADVANTAGE...

SIZE ADVANTAGE? BUT WE'RE MUCH BIGGER...

NO, SMALL IS BETTER, FASTER. THEY CAN VANISH THROUGH A CHINK IN THE WALL. THEY CAN ALSO SEE AT NIGHT AS WELL AS IN DAYLIGHT.

DOC, YOU'RE STARTING TO SCARE ME.

YOU BETTER BE SCARED. BECAUSE THESE RATS WE'VE MADE, THIS NEW SPECIES, IS HOSTILE TO US. WE DON'T KNOW WHY. SOONER OR LATER SOMEONE WOULD HAVE BEEN KILLED IF WE HADN'T TAKEN EXTREME PRECAUTIONS.

DOOFUS, GET IN HERE. RIGHT NOW!

THATTA BOY, DOOFUS. EVERYTHING'S FINE.

WE'LL DRIVE TO BIOLOMECH. WE'LL TELL THEM WE'VE FOUND...

RRRRR

WHAT'S WRONG, MOM?

RRRR

THE JEEP WON'T START, TOMMY.

THIS IS HOW THEY GOT OUT UNDER THE FENCE. THEY GOT TO THE OTHER SIDE AND...ESCAPED. THEY'RE OUT THERE SOMEWHERE...RUNNING FREE.

ONE OF YOU NAMED PARNELL? SHERIFF ASKED ME TO BRING YOU THIS BLOODHOUND.

AND SO BEN LED THE DESPERATE SEARCH TO FIND THE MUTATED RATS...

THE LIGHT REVEALED A MESS OF TORN AND TANGLED WIRES. HOLES HAD BEEN GNAWED IN THE HOSES. SHE WAS NO LONGER JUST SCARED...SHE WAS FLAT-OUT TERRIFIED!

I DON'T KNOW WHAT'S WRONG, BUT IT'S DEAD.

THE RATS GOT TO IT, DIDN'T THEY?

RATS? WELL, THEY'RE IN THE HOUSE, YES, BUT--

YOU'RE TRYING NOT TO SHOW IT, BUT YOU'RE REALLY AFRAID OF THEM, WHICH MUST MEAN THEY'RE NOT JUST DIFFERENT. YOU WERE SCARED WHEN DAD DIED, BUT NOT FOR LONG.

BUT THESE RATS, WHATEVER THEY ARE, THEY SCARE YOU MORE THAN ANYTHING HAS. I'VE BEEN THINKING...THEY'RE AWFUL SMART, AND NOW THEY'VE GOT THE JEEP. WHAT ARE WE GOING TO DO?

WE'LL GO BACK TO THE HOUSE. I'VE GOT TO USE THE PHONE.

THEY'LL HAVE THOUGHT OF THE PHONE.

MAYBE, BUT HOW SMART CAN THEY BE?

SMART ENOUGH TO THINK OF THE JEEP.

THE FLOOR BUCKED, THROWING MEG OFF HER FEET.

FIRE LICKED UP THE WALLS, SPREAD ACROSS THE FLOOR, STARTING TO CUT HER OFF FROM THE DOOR.

SHE SAW THAT A PIECE OF BROKEN GLASS HAD STUCK IN HER HAND.

SHE TORE THE GLASS FROM HER HAND, THE PAIN OVERWHELMING.

BLINDLY, KNOWING SHE HAD ONLY MOMENTS LEFT, SHE STUMBLED TO THE DOOR.

MEG WENT TO THE BARN ALONE. THE RATS WOULD BE THERE. THE PIECE OF GLASS HAD LEFT HER WITH ONLY ONE GOOD HAND BUT SHE WOULD STILL KILL ALL THE RATS...

MORE IMPORTANT, IT WAS THE ONLY PLACE WHERE SHE AND TOMMY HAD A HOPE OF SURVIVING THE NIGHT.

HURRY, MEN!

HE KNEW THE RATS HAD CAUSED THE FIRE. HE DID NOT KNOW HOW OR WHY.

HORRIBLE IMAGES PLAYED IN HIS MIND. THE WOMAN AND THE BOY, THEIR RAT-GNAWED BODIES AFLAME IN THE MIDDLE OF THE HOUSE.

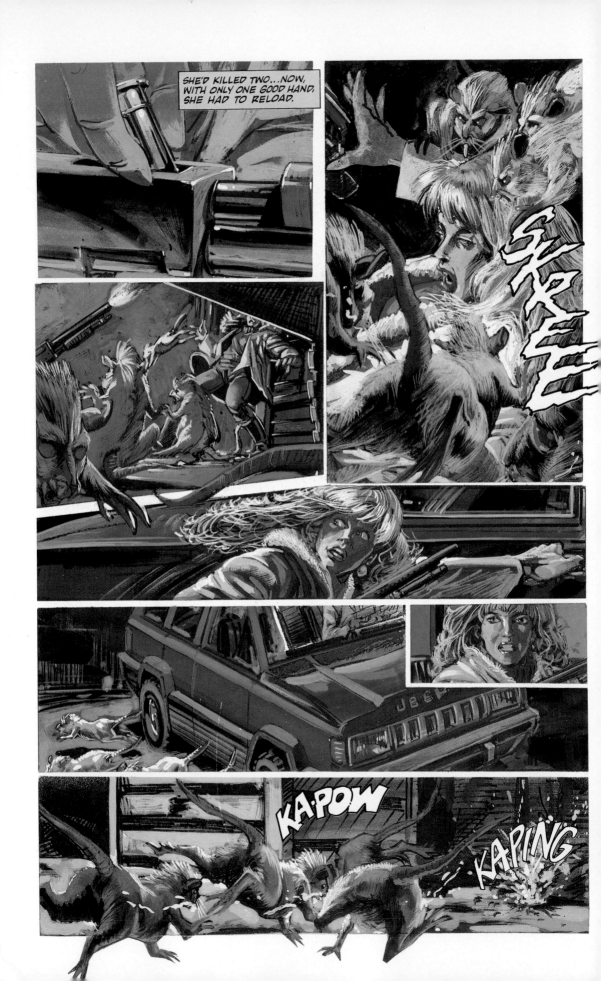

GET OUT OF THE WAY!

K-POW
K-POW

K-POW

K-POW

ARE YOU ALL RIGHT, MRS. LASSITER?

HOW MANY ARE THEY? I KILLED FOUR AND YOU KILLED ONE, SO HOW MANY ARE LEFT?

JUST THOSE THREE. HEY, YOUR HAND'S BLEEDING...

THEY'RE FOUL MONSTERS, AND I WANT TO FINISH THEM ALL, MAKE THEM PAY FOR TAKING MY HOME, BUT HOW CAN WE GET AT THEM DOWN IN THE GROUND?

I THINK MAYBE THEY'VE GOT A TUNNEL BETWEEN THE BARN AND THE HOUSE. I'VE GOT A HUNCH IT IS AT THE BOTTOM OF THAT FEED BIN.

WE FIGURED WHEN WE FOUND THE RATS, THEY MIGHT BE BURROWED IN. WE HAVE THE EQUIPMENT TO PUMP GAS DOWN THEIR HOLE.

I WANT THEM DEAD.

WE GAVE 'EM A GENEROUS DOSE. ENOUGH TO SATURATE A BURROW TEN TIMES LARGER THAN ANY THEY'VE HAD TIME TO DIG.

NOW WE'LL EXCAVATE. WE'LL START STRIPPING THE SURFACE OFF THE GROUND, DIGGING BACKWARDS FROM THE BARN WALL UNTIL WE TURN THEM UP.

AND IF YOU DON'T TURN THEM UP?

WE WILL. I'M SURE WE WILL.

MEG WANTED TO HATE HIM, BECAUSE HE WAS THE ONLY FIGURE OF AUTHORITY SHE COULD VENT HER ANGER ON. BUT HE WAS RESPONSIBLE FOR THE RATS. FURTHERMORE SHE WAS TOUCHED BY HIS GENUINE SYMPATHY WHEN SHE TOLD HIM HER HUSBAND HAD DIED.

HE SPOKE OF LOSS AND LONELINESS AND LONGING AS IF HE HAD HAD HIS SHARE OF THEM.

I GUESS THEY WEREN'T ALL *THAT* SMART, BOSS.

I THOUGHT MAYBE YOU'D WANT TO SEE THEM--THAT WE'VE GOT ALL EIGHT, I MEAN.

I WOULD, YES. I'LL FEEL SAFER.

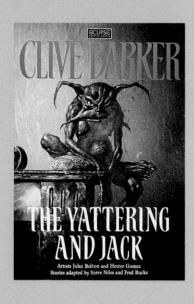

CLIVE BARKER'S

THE YATTERING AND JACK

Adapted by Steve Niles
Illustrated by John Bolton

A DARKLY HILARIOUS and weirdly perceptive tale of the devil at work from the acclaimed fantasist and master of horror fiction, Clive Barker.

Beelzebub sends his underling the Yattering to claim the soul of Jack Polo, pickle salesman. But in the Polo residence where the Yattering is bound, nothing doing. Polo's response, even to disaster, is merely to sigh, '*Que sera sera*'. The Yattering is going crazy. He must goad Polo to lunacy, the Old One insists. Polo was promised by his mother to the Lord of the Flies. And what match is a chronically dull pickle salesman for hell's own spawn . . . ? Find out.

Included in the same volume, a graphic adaptation of Clive Barker's short story *How Spoilers Bleed,* adapted by Steve Niles and Fred Burke, and illustrated by Hector Gomez. It tells of the gory revenge visited on white destroyers of the Brazilian jungle by the dying indigenous people of the Amazon basin. It is a punishment that fits the crime, incredibly unpleasant . . .

Clive Barker's bestselling works of fiction include *The Books of Blood, The Damnation Game, Weaveworld, Cabal, The Great and Secret Show, The Hellbound Heart , Imajica* and *The Thief of Always*. Not only is he prodigiously talented as a writer, he also produces and directs memorable films such as the *Hellraiser* trilogy, *Nightbreed* and *Candyman*, and is himself a spectacular visual artist. The illustrators he chooses to work with, therefore, John Bolton and Hector Gomez, are equally brilliant.

NEIL GAIMAN

MIRACLEMAN: THE GOLDEN AGE

Illustrated by Mark Buckingham

NEIL GAIMAN'S spectacular, mysterious, luminously strange and compelling saga of the all-British superhero and deity, Miracleman. *The Golden Age* is the age of miracles unimagined. It is the age of gods among men. It is the age of truth in which everything is what it seems, and nothing is as it was imagined.

'A work that transforms the superhero genre into something strange, wonderful, and politic. Excellent stuff!'

ALAN MOORE

MIRACLEMAN was given new life by Alan Moore, known as the King of the graphic novel, in the early 1980s. His and Gaiman's work is assessed in the critique below by Samuel R. Delany, author of *Dhalgren*, the *Nevèrÿon* series, and other science fiction masterpieces.

'Moore and Gaiman are the two writers who have done more to change the idea of what comics are and can be than anyone since . . . well, certainly since I started reading them in the 1940s. Reading Moore, followed by Gaiman, I found myself for the first time deeply, consistently, intensely interested in these comic book writers *as writers*. With that interest came a revision in the idea of what comics could be; they could be *written*, not just in a craftsman-like manner adequate to the visuals. The writing could be brilliant in itself. Here were writers with the range of language from silence to song - the whole of language with which to put across their stories. And the stories themselves! Gaiman's six entwined tales in *The Golden Age* come like sapphires afloat on a super-cooled liquid. They unfold like haiku. The voices they speak with are real. Their lambent characters, yearning both for bits of yesterday and portents of tomorrow, will linger with you long.'

SAMUEL R. DELANY

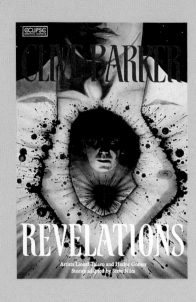

CLIVE BARKER'S

REVELATIONS

Adapted by Steve Niles
Illustrated by Lionel Talaro

ANOTHER CLIVE BARKER story of living mayhem and dying faith adapted for the graphic form by Steve Niles and illustrated by Lionel Talaro.

A murder thirty years ago, to the night, haunts the motel room where it happened - and where evangelist John Gyer and his unhappy wife Virginia are staying. Virginia senses the ghosts of Buck and Sadie Durning are near. But her dependence on pills to alleviate the oppressive effect her husband's "goodness" has on her lead her only to hideous dreams of violence. Observing her, the ghost Sadie, who was executed for the murder of her husband, is moved to sympathy. She is unrepentant, even though tonight she and the ghost of her husband have returned to the Cottonwood Motel to attempt a reconciliation beyond the grave. Virginia's problem is more compelling to her than Buck's lustful ghost. Before the clouds part to reveal a full moon, the blood-letting, the inevitable tragedy, will come to pass, again.

Clive Barker, the supreme fantasist, mixes life and death in a heady cocktail. Included in the same volume, an adaptation of his sinister story, *Babel's Children*, illustrated by Hector Gomez and adapted by Steve Niles.